For contact via our web site: www.plantingseedstoday.com

Planting Seeds

Stories by
Barry Gearin

Illustrations by Pam G. Jones

REFLECTIONS

 Please read these stories many times, and over time, to your children. Find other stories to read and make up a few of your own along the way: a beginning, middle and end. It's not that hard. Describe the hero somewhat, but don't name who it might be.

 Slow way down at bedtime and other times, too. Really focus in on your child. One never knows when a special moment will occur. But when it does, the memory and the feeling will last forever.

 Socrates said a virtue is not innate, it is learned. It is nurtured through young developing morals. If, as adults, we are the sum total of all our experiences, then it is reasoned, the childhood foundation is so very important. This critical point in time sets the ball rolling for all that we will become. Plant good seeds now while the foundation is fertile.

 Children learn from what they hear, but learn so much more from what they observe.

Table of Contents

Crossing the Street..............................1

The Stranger.................................5

The Treasure Chest.........................11

Angel in the Attic...........................19

The Bus Trip 25

Boo Bear 33

The Starfish................................. 41

Ten Colors....................................45

A Children's Prayer.......................53

A Moment is Made 55
a poem for mom and dad

Crossing the Street

So there they were, just like they were the day before: a father teaching his son to cross the street all by himself. "Geez, Dad, this is easy. Why do we have to go over the same stuff we did yesterday?"

"Because I want to make sure you do it right. Check one way, then the other. **Then do it again…** check one way and then the other, then hurry across the street."

"Two times. Geez, come on, Dad, I get it," said Tommy.

The next day Tommy saw his friends on the other side of the street. "Come on over," they all yelled. Tommy looked both ways twice and then he hurried across the street, just like he had practiced with his dad.

His friends on the other side of the street laughed. "We only check once before we cross." Tyler spoke up too. "Sometimes I don't even look at all. Nothing's going to happen to me. I got the power."

While all this was happening, Tommy's dad was watching through the kitchen window. Tommy ran back across the street. He only looked once. At that very moment, Tommy's dad became very upset. He went into his bedroom, took off his pants and changed into shorts. He then came outside to see all the boys.

From a distance, one of the boys said, "Look, Tommy, here comes your dad. I've never seen him in shorts before or even in a bathing suit." As he got closer, they could all see the most hideous scar they had ever seen. *Tommy's dad's leg was so scary.* It was so ugly. It was hard to even look at. No one said a word.

His dad sat down on the curb and said slowly, "See this scar? When I was six years old, I crossed a very busy street. I looked both ways only once. Not twice. *BAM… I never saw it coming.* The truck hit me so hard I was knocked up into the sky and fell back down…and was knocked out. I almost died. I worried my mom and dad so very much.

"So, whenever I see anyone, like good boys in the neighborhood, or my son, cross a street without looking twice, I get scared their leg might look like my leg." The boys just stared at his leg.

"Will you boys always look twice?"

They all yelled, "YES, YES, WE WILL, WE WILL."

"You promise?"

"Yes, yes, we will."

"Okay," said Tommy's dad. "What do you say we all go swimming together? Everybody get their swimsuits on and meet back right here."

"And remember…… "

They all nodded.

THE END

The Stranger

It was a sunny afternoon. School was already out for the day. And a little girl named Sarah was out playing in her front yard. Sarah was a very happy and friendly little girl. Her hair was filled with big red curls and she always seemed to be smiling.

At about this time, a very big man came walking down the sidewalk. He noticed the little girl doing cartwheels on the grass. He bent down on one knee and waved for her to come on over.

He seemed nice so Sarah ran over to him. He told her she might win a gold medal in the Olympics some day. "Those cartwheels are just about perfect," he said.

Just then, Sarah's mom appeared in the doorway. **She had the look of terror upon her face.** She was afraid Sarah was about to be taken away by the stranger. Sarah's mom thought she recognized him but was not sure. She waited a moment as the stranger began to speak.

"Well, little girl, I have to return these DVD movies at the store just down there around the corner. Would you like to come with me?" said the man with the scruffy beard.

Sarah thought… then said, "Maybe… Okay, I'll go."

The man was surprised, almost shocked at her answer. He then asked

another question. "Do you know what a stranger is?"

"I forgot," said Sarah.

"Hasn't your mom or dad told you about strangers?"

"I forgot," she said.

"Well," said the man. "A stranger is someone you don't really know.

A stranger is also someone your mommy or daddy doesn't know.

Do you understand?"

"Kind of……I think," said Sarah cautiously.

"That doesn't sound like you're sure of it to me. Here, let's do a test," said
the man. "You know what a test is, don't you?"

"Yes, I do, of course I do," said Sarah confidently.

"Okay, then let's take this test. Ready? Oh, I almost forgot. You take this test up in your head. ***There are three questions.*** And you ask them to yourself. Nobody else is supposed to hear the questions. Do you understand?"

"Yes, I sure do," Sarah said.

"Okay, question number one: ***do you know my name?*** And remember, up in your head." The stranger could see Sarah thinking. "Question number two: ***have you ever seen me before?***" He waited another moment… "and question number three: ***does your mom or dad know my name?***"

"Test is over. If you answer ***NO*** to these three questions then ***I AM A STRANGER.***" He paused, then asked, "What do you do now?"

She looked confused. "Think," he said. "Think hard."

"I got it. I don't know your name and I've never seen you before." Sarah started to run very fast to her front door.

"Hey, where are you going?"

"Question number three," she yelled. "I need to know if my mom or dad knows your name!"

"Mommy, mommy!" Sarah ran through the front door. "Mommy, I met a new man. I mean, I met a stranger I think. Come quick, see if you know his name. Hurry!"

When they got outside the stranger was gone. He had left to return his DVDs. Sarah's mom held her hands and looked into her eyes. "Sarah, honey, was he a stranger?"

"Yes, he was," Sarah said firmly. "And if I'm alone, I will not talk to a stranger. I know what a stranger is now." Sarah's mom hugged her so tight. She was so proud of her big girl.

Later that night as they sat together at the dinner table, Sarah's dad spoke up. "I hear we have a new neighbor. A new man moved in a few houses down the street."

Mom smiled. "I cannot wait to meet him!"

Sarah smiled, too. "Yes, Daddy, that way he won't be a stranger anymore."

They all smiled at the same time and then Sarah asked what was for dessert.

THE END

The Treasure Chest

Once upon a time, in a neighborhood not too far from here, lived three little boys. Actually, they weren't so little. They were growing bigger and stronger every day. Then one day, a new boy moved into the neighborhood. The three good friends wondered if the new boy would become their new friend.

His name was Andy and he had just moved into the very old house at the end of the street. After his family got all settled in, Andy ventured to the far corner of his new big back yard. The other three boys were peering in quietly through the back yard gate.

Andy could not believe his eyes. For under the branches and brambles and fallen leaves, there sat a real-life treasure chest. At first, he thought it was some kind of toy chest, but it was heavy and it looked so real. On the top of the chest it read, "Open only if you can live by the Code of Loyalty."

"Code of Loyalty," he said to himself. *"What does that mean?"*

"It means always be ready to help a friend. And maybe…to even die in battle for a friend."

"Who said that?" yelled Andy.

"I did," yelled back Dillon.

Just then, the three boys walked up behind Andy and right next to the amazing new treasure chest. They opened it up slowly. Inside were four swords. On each handle it read, **"LOYALTY FOREVER."** Also, on each sword, and this was the amazing part, it read each of their names, ANDY and DILLON on two of them. Andy read the other two names out loud, "BRIAN and CHRIS."

"Hey, that's us!" exclaimed the other two boys. They all pulled out their own swords very carefully. The swords were so sharp. They were really real. Each one could cut down a thick tree with one swing. They started to play. They started to sword fight. They all realized these must be magic swords because, no matter how hard they fought, they never hit each other's bodies. For if they did, globs of blood would surely spurt out from their bellies.

No, these swords were magical. The boys fought long and hard. They pretended they were pirates fighting over buried treasure. Then they were brave knights saving the queen from evil enemies. The boys played and pretended for hours. A little later, it was time for dinner. The swords were placed back into the treasure chest as they all yelled out, *"Loyalty Forever!"*

The next day at school, Brian got into the wrong line by mistake. Instead of helping him, Chris told the teacher on him. Brian was mad at Chris, and later that day at recess, Brian hit him in the face with the tether ball. *"OUCH! That hurt,"* cried out Chris.

After school, the four boys were back at the treasure chest. They opened it up together but there were only two swords, Andy and Dillon's. *"HEY, how come our swords are missing?"* cried the other two boys. They could not understand and ran home crying. Meanwhile, Andy and Dillon played until the sun went down.

The next day in school, the teacher gave a really hard test. Dillon couldn't figure out the answers by himself. So you know what he did? He looked over Andy's shoulder and cheated and stole the answers.

Later that day, the four boys opened the heavy chest together. But only one sword remained. Guess which one? It was Andy's. He took it out and began to play. He swung it through the air. *It was faster than the wind.* But he had no one to play with. He began to get upset.

"I thought you were my new friends when I moved in. You guys aren't such good friends. One of you cheated on me on my test. And Brian and Chris hurt each other at school. Out of my yard! *Everybody get out of my yard!* Why should I be loyal to guys like you? Get out, you bums, " yelled Andy.

Andy was more than mad. He was being mean. Andy's mom called him inside for a pudding break. After his snack, he ran back outside to play. He opened up the chest and could not believe his eyes. *"Oh no,"* he yelled. *"Now all the swords are gone!"*

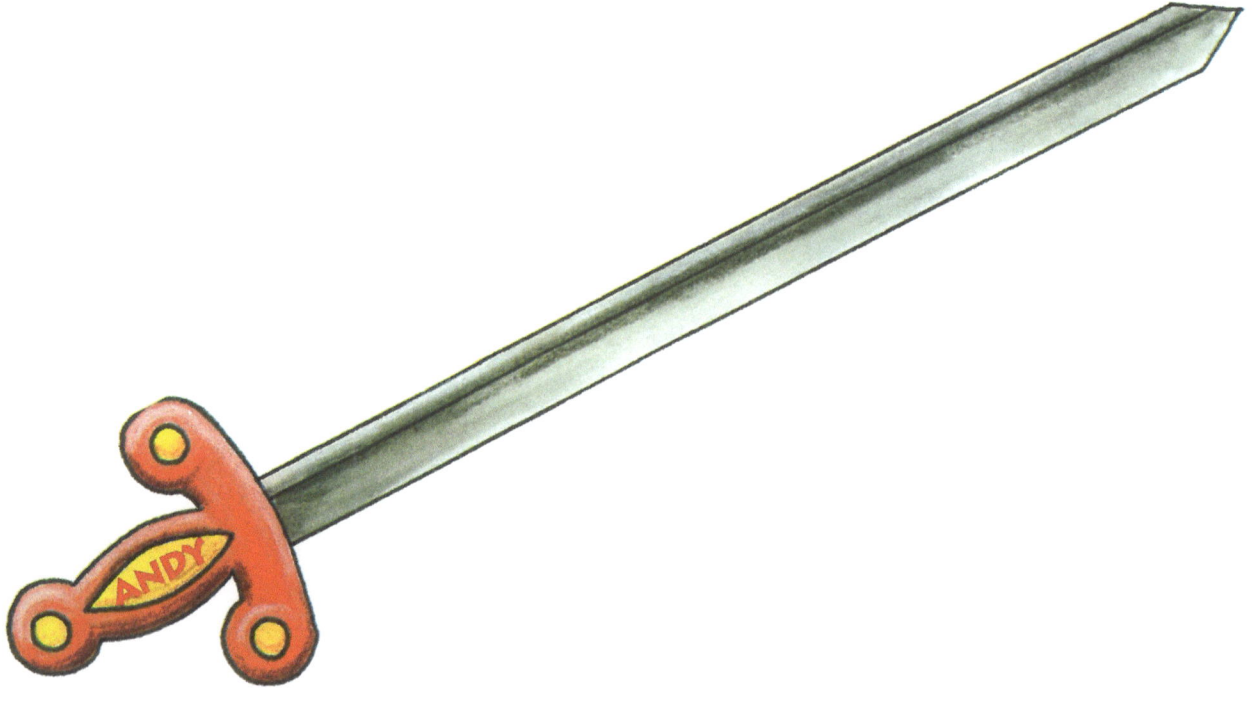

The next day, the four boys were walking home together. They were all so very sad. They were quiet for a really long time. Then Brian spoke up. "Hey Chris, I'm sorry I hit you in the face with the ball. That must have really hurt."

"I guess I'm sorry, too, for not helping you get into the right line."

"And I won't cheat on any more tests. I can do things on my own." said Dillon.

"I should not have yelled and been so mean," said Andy. "Friends should not act that way to each other or else they are not really friends." Just then Andy had an idea. "Hey, guys, no matter what happens we will always be friends. We will always help each other and we'll always be loyal, just like real knights on horses. Okay, what do you say?" They all put their four hands together and yelled, *"LOYALTY FOREVER!"*

Back in Andy's back yard, someone asked, "What should we do with the treasure chest?"

"I guess I could use it as a toy chest and put all my toys in it," said Andy.

The boys opened up the chest and could not believe their eyes. The four swords were magically back inside. They were all so happy again, sword fighting and yelling out, *"FRIENDS FOREVER and LOYALTY FOREVER!"* None of them had naps that day. They played and played and played.

THE END

Angel in the Attic

She had beautiful wings. Really big wings. And she had a shiny gold belt and a long white fluffy gown. Oh, and her face was so beautiful. This is how Rebecca was describing what she had just seen to her little brother, Todd.

Her little brother could not believe this crazy story. "Listen Rebecca, you've got to be fooling with me, playing a joke on me," said Todd.

"No, no," said Rebecca. *"It was real. I think she's an angel.* And she kept pointing to the old dusty phone up in the attic. But I got scared and that's when I ran down here to you."

Todd thought about this for a moment and then said, "Okay, Rebecca, I believe you." And with that, they both started up the squeaky steps. Old pictures and clothes, dusty books and a few cob webs covered Grandma's attic. As they got half way up, Todd asked, "You sure you want to go back up here?"

"Yeah, we've got to pick up that phone."

"Okay," said Todd a bit nervously as they got closer and closer to the top step.

Two weeks ago, Rebeccas and Todd's Grandma died and went up to Heaven. The two kids were so sad. But they remembered what she said to them while she lay on her big fluffy bed. She looked deep into their eyes and held their hands. She smiled big, like Grandma always did, and said, "I'm getting old. I've had so much fun down here with both of you. I've had a long, good life, and now it's time to go." She closed her eyes and then she died.

That was two weeks ago. And now they were in the attic walking toward the phone. Todd went to pick it up and Rebecca said, *"No, wait! The angel wanted me to pick up the phone."*

She picked up the phone and held it to her ear. To her amazement, it began to ring. Todd said, "How can that be? It's not even plugged in. And look here, Rebecca, the cord to the phone is cut." But it was ringing all right. They both had goose bumps. Four rings. Five rings. And then suddenly… someone picked up the phone.

21

"Hello. Who's calling, please?" asked a very cheerful voice.

"Uh..uh…It's Rebecca and Todd."

"Marvelous. We've been expecting your call."

"WHAT!" exclaimed Rebecca. *"YOU KNEW WE WOULD CALL?"*

"Of course. This is Heaven you're calling. Hold on just one moment, please," said the cheerful voice.

"Hey, Todd! It's Heaven we're calling!"

"Yeah, right," said Todd. Rebecca held the phone so they both could listen in. They waited and waited. And then…

"Hello, hello, my sweeties. I love you. I love you so very much."

"GRANDMA! Hello, hello Grandma. We love you and we miss you. Can you come back?"

"Oh no," said Grandma. "I cannot do that."

"Can we come visit you?"

"I'm afraid not, my sweeties. Heaven doesn't work that way."

"What's Heaven like?" asked Todd. "Can you tell us, Grandma?"

"Well, I'm not supposed to tell you much about this place. God wants us to keep it a secret. You remember what secrets are. Oh, but I can tell you this. It's the most beautiful and fun place you could ever dream of.

"Also," said Grandma, "we won't be able to talk again until it's time for you to come up, which won't be until you are as old as me."

Todd and Rebecca were silent. "Don't worry, my sweeties. You have lots and lots of pictures of us together. And we will always love each other wherever we are, right?"

Just then the beautiful angel appeared off to the side. The angel wasn't touching the ground. She was floating above the floor, smiling. Grandma said, "I have a present for both of you. This guardian angel watched over me my whole life, protecting me from danger and I didn't even know it. Now, she will always watch over you and protect you."

"WOW. This is neat, Grandma. What a present!" they both exclaimed.

"Now, don't forget to say your prayers tonight and every night. Do you know why?"

"Why, Grandma, why?"

"There's one secret up here in Heaven I think I can tell you. Want to know the secret?"

"Yes, yes of course, Grandma!"

"Ready? Here it is. The more you say your prayers, and the more you are thankful for all the things you already have, the more the angels are allowed to watch over you and ***bless you with even more good things.***"

"Wow, what a great secret!"

Grandma said, "I've got to go now. I love you both so much. Good-bye for now."

Later that night, after they said their prayers, Rebecca and Todd lay their tired heads upon their big fluffy pillows. They fell asleep smiling, so happy that Grandma's angel was now watching over them.

THE END

The Bus Trip

His long hard journey was done. He stepped off the bus and into the rushing arms of his son.

"Father, father, you made it back in time for my birthday!" said Randy very excitedly.

"Of course. I would never miss my big boy's big birthday party."

"Father, father, can I go on your next bus trip? Can I, can I go?"

Randy's father took a deep breath and said, "We'll see, son. Like I've said before, when I think you're ready for this kind of bus trip, I will surely take you along. But right now, we have to get home and help your mother fix up the house for the big birthday celebration."

The next day was Randy's birthday. He sat proudly in the big birthday seat as all his friends began to arrive. Randy was a very lucky young man, for he had lots and lots of friends.

Games and play time, cake and goodies filled the day. Then it was time for the presents. There were lots of presents, more than most kids see in a whole year. Randy began to open his gifts, slowly at first, then faster and faster. He would open a very nice gift quickly, smile, and then race on to the next gift. He did not realize how long it took to shop for a nice gift and take special care to wrap it just right.

When he was all done, he jumped up from the table and yelled out, *"LAST ONE IN THE POOL IS A ROTTEN EGG!"*

Randy never noticed the sad look on his parent's face. "Wow, so many gifts and **he never said one thank you**," said his mother.

"I think Randy may be too lucky," said his dad. "Wow, not one thank you."

A few days passed. It was a beautiful morning. The sun shone brightly into Randy's bedroom. He was just waking up as his father sat down on the bed, bringing news of a big surprise.

"Father, father, what is it? Oh, what could it be?"

"Well, the next bus leaves in two hours. You are now ready for the bus trip. You're invited if you'd like to come."

"Yes, yes, of course," shouted Randy as he started to dress.

The bus left at noon. There were lots of big people on the bus. In fact, all were big except for Randy... He felt proud. As he looked around, he noticed lots and lots of clothes and big boxes of food. In the back of the bus were blankets and used shoes. He wondered out loud to himself, "Geez, why so many shoes?"

The ride was long. He slowly closed his eyes and fell asleep. After a while, the road became bumpy. "Wake up son, we're almost there."

27

Randy was so excited. He was the first one off the bus. "Wow! Look, father. Look at all the clubhouses. They're just like the one you made for me and my friends to play in. Neat."

"No, son, these are homes. Families live in them," said his father.

"But they're so small. Some even have holes in the roof."

After a while, Randy settled in. He helped his father and the others work in the village. He met lots of new friends his age. They all liked his brand new shoes. "I got them at my birthday party."

"What is a birthday party?" asked two boys and a girl at the same time.

Randy was so surprised. ***"You don't know what a birthday party is?*** A birthday party is…"

Just then his father interrupted and said he had to take some clothes down to the next village. "You'll be safe with Rosa and her kids. I'll be back in a little while."

"Hurry back," said Randy. "Hurry back." Randy worked and he played and he played and he worked. Hours had passed and his father had not returned.

"Don't worry, Randy," said Rosa. "Your father will be just fine. That old bus sometimes gives us all a few problems. He'll be fine. Come on everyone. It's time for dinner."

After dinner, Randy asked, *"What's for dessert?"*

All the boys and girls looked at him kind of funny. "What is a dessert?" asked the quiet boy with no shoes on his feet.

Randy was so surprised to learn they never had dessert or even knew what it was.

"Let's go, everyone. Time for bed," yelled out Rosa. She tucked all the kids in to bed, including a very tired and worried Randy. "Don't forget to all say your prayers," said a very loving Rosa.

Back at the other village, the old bus had, in fact, broken down. Randy's father needed to wait until the morning to fix the bus. He needed the morning sunlight because there were no lights in this very poor village.

Randy was now cuddled up in the small bed with four other children. He tried to say his prayers, but he started to cry. He was sad. Back home he had his very own bed and his own bedroom. He always had dessert and everyone he knew had nice shoes. Most of all, he missed his father. "Please, God, help my father to get back safely. I really, really miss him. And please, God, help these poor people." He finally fell asleep.

When Randy woke up, it was sunny and his father had returned. "Hey, big boy. It's almost time for our long journey back home. Why don't you say good-bye to all your new friends." Randy nodded and smiled, and then gave his father the longest, tightest hug.

On the bus, Randy hung his head out the window and waved good-bye to all his new friends. Randy's father looked down at his son's bare feet. "Son, *where are your brand new birthday shoes?*"

Randy just smiled and pointed out the window. A little boy was smiling and laughing and waving back at his new best friend. He wasn't so quiet anymore. He was wearing brand new shoes.

When they got back home, Randy ran right past his mother, who was cooking a big dinner. "Where on earth are you rushing off to?" called his mother.

"I've got lots of phone calls to make."

"Why?" said his mother and father at the same time.

"To call all my friends and thank them for all the great gifts they gave me.
And to ask them all if they have any extra shoes for the next bus trip."

Randy never noticed the very happy and proud smiles on his parents' faces.
"Wow," they both said together. "Wow."

THE END

Boo Bear

"It's time for bed, sweetheart."

"Okay. Mommy, but could you leave the light on?" asked Kara. "And could you leave the door open? Wide open!"

"Yes, of course, my little sweetie," said Kara's mom. "And don't forget to say your prayers."

Kara's dad stood in the doorway, smiling at his little girl. "You know, sweetheart, there is nothing to be afraid of."

After they said goodnight and walked down the long hallway, Kara wondered if she would always be afraid of the dark. She became sleepy. **But then, she heard something moving around.** It was under her bed. No, wait. It was in her closet. She began to tremble with fear. Oh no, there was a monster right in her bedroom!

Just then, she heard kind of a soothing voice. "You won't always be like this, you know. You won't always be afraid."

"Who said…Where are…What…Where..." Kara was so scared.

Then Kara focused her eyes on her little rocking chair in the corner. He was sitting in the chair like he always did.

"Boo Bear, is that you? My cuddle bear, my toy bear talking to me?"

"It is me. Your Boo Bear. I sit right here, watching you while you sleep every night. I wish I could say I protect you, but nothing ever happens, no matter how dark it gets."

"You're alive! You can speak!" But how? You didn't speak at the toy store," said an amazed Kara.

"I know. I know. None of us bears can speak at the toy store. Only some of us can come alive when we are really needed by little children." Boo Bear and Kara talked and talked. Boo Bear even jumped up onto the bed. After a while, he cuddled up next to Kara and they both fell asleep.

At about seven o'clock in the morning, Kara's mom came into the bedroom. "Good morning Ka....hey, how did Boo Bear get in there?"

"Good morning, Mommy. Guess what? Boo Bear can talk. And he helped me get to sleep last night. Get Daddy, please... hurry."

As Kara's mom went to get her dad, Boo Bear leaned over and whispered in Kara's ear, "I can only come alive for you."

"But why, Boo Bear?"

"Because you're the only one here that needs me. You're the only one in the house that's afraid of the dark." Just then, Kara's mom and dad walked into the room. Boo Bear stopped talking just in time. He was almost caught. And no parent, as far as we know, has ever heard a Boo Bear talking.

"Now what's this about a talking Boo Bear?" asked Daddy.

Kara thought for a moment. She wanted so badly to tell them both the whole story. But how could she? How would they ever believe her, she thought, especially if Boo Bear was not going to say a word? "Oh well," she said. "Maybe I was still dreaming." And with that, she let out a big, long yaaaawn.

At breakfast and lunch and even at dinner, Boo Bear would play funny tricks. When Kara's mom or dad would look away or get up from the table, Boo Bear would wink or smile or even wave his hands way up in the air. And sometimes he would even speak up. ***"Could I have some more milk, please?"***

Mom would turn around. "But honey, you have a full glass of milk already." Boo Bear, very quietly, would be laughing to himself. He was quite a joker.

At bedtime, he would joke with Kara, making her smile and laugh. Eventually Kara looked forward to bedtime. Sometimes Mom and Dad heard giggles coming from Kara's bedroom.

"To think, Boo Bear, I used to be afraid of the dark. But I'm not afraid anymore. You know, the night is really just the same as the daytime."

"Oh yeah, how is that so?" asked a confused Boo Bear.

"Well," said Kara, "when its nighttime here, its daytime on the other side of the world. Sometimes I think of that and I fall asleep. That's, of course, when you're not making me laugh and giggle."

Over time, Boo Bear and Kara became such good friends. They played and played when nobody else was looking, of course. A few birthdays went by and nobody knew their secret. After a while, Kara was not afraid of anything. At school, she would sit in the front row and raise her hand to answer any question with confidence. At school and with her friends, she became quite a leader.

At about this time, she was invited to go to her little cousin's birthday party. Little Joseph was about to turn three years old.

Boo Bear loved parties and asked if he could go. "Boo Bear," said Kara, "I'm almost six. I really shouldn't be bringing a bear out to a party."

Boo Bear began to get a little tear. It wasn't a toy tear. It was a real tear.

"I'm sorry, Boo Bear. That was rude of me. Of course you can come."

At Joseph's birthday party, there were lots of gifts. The final gift was a special gift from his mom and dad. It was a big boy lamp for his bedroom.

"Wow, Joseph," said his dad. "You won't be afraid of the dark anymore with a lamp like this."

"I don't know, Dad. It still is dark and scary outside," said a very nervous little boy. "And you know, Mom, a lamp can't protect you from nighttime monsters."

Joseph needed a friend so he wouldn't be scared anymore. Boo Bear and Kara looked at each other from across the room. They both knew what had to be done. At this very moment, they were both happy and sad. Happy because they could both help someone who really needed help, and sad because they both knew what that meant, a sad good-bye.

When everyone was still around Joseph, Kara and Boo Bear hugged each other for a long time. "Kara, this means I won't be able to talk to you again!" said Boo Bear.

"Yes, you will. Joseph lives close by. I can visit lots."

"Yes, but I can only come alive for one child at a time."

Kara did not think of this. For a moment, it really concerned her. But she thought about this for a while longer, gave Boo Bear another long hug and then spoke up. "Joseph, there is one more present for you. His name is Boo Bear. And he is a very, very special bear."

The party was coming to an end. As Kara and her parents were heading for the front door, Kara's mom told her, "That was a very special thing you did for Joseph. I know Boo Bear meant a lot to you. Joseph is a lucky boy."

"Yes....and so is Boo Bear. He gets to help two kids grow up."

From a distance, Kara saw Joseph hugging Boo Bear. Kara waved good-bye. Boo Bear was hugging Joseph tightly with one paw. The other paw was waving back. Nobody else saw.

THE END

The Starfish

Once upon a time, a father and his son were walking along a beautiful beach. As the day was ending and the sun drifted down toward the ocean, a very smart little boy taught his dad a valuable lesson.

He taught his dad something so special that **both of them would never forget this lesson.**

As they walked along the soft white sand, leaving behind lots and lots of footprints, they came upon a starfish. As the tide was drifting back out to sea, the starfish struggled and struggled to inch his way back so that a wave might carry him to where he would live to see another day.

The boy bent down to pick up the starfish, help him along, and of course, save his life.

"Son, what are you doing?" asked the boy's dad. "Listen here. Before you do that, stand up and look and see what I see."

He did stand up. "Yes, what do you see, Dad?"

His dad pointed down the beach, "Look, son, as far as we both can see, every so many feet, another starfish struggles to get back to the sea."

The boy looked down at the one starfish in front of him.

"And, son, we cannot help all of these poor starfish," said his dad. "It will take days and days."

The boy looked down at the sad, sad starfish and then back up to his dad. "Yes, Dad, I know I cannot help all the starfish. But I know I can really make a big difference for this one here."

His dad was speechless. He realized his son was right.

And with that, the little boy gently picked up the starfish and put him back to sea. And, of course, he made one very big difference for one very happy starfish.

Later, as they both rode home on their bicycles, the father admitted to his son, "You know, back at the beach, you taught me one of the best lessons that I have ever learned. ***That it is better to help one that you can than none at all.***"

"That's right, Dad. And guess what else?"

"What, son?"

"Maybe I can help more. Maybe I can convince my teacher to have a field trip at the beach. We have 25 kids in class. That's 25 starfish we can help."

"Wow," said his dad. "Wow."

"And maybe, just maybe, my teacher can talk the principal into letting all the classes come down here. ***That's so many kids I can't count that high!***"

"Son, you taught me so much today."

"Just think, Dad, tomorrow's another day."

THE END

Ten Colors

The rain was coming down harder now. Deshawn was watching the big round raindrops slide down the window pane. It sure looked like there would be no outside recess today.

The teacher gave some fun assignments and some work assignments. But as the day wore on, she noticed the class becoming more and more restless. Little quarrels and fights were beginning to break out.

"Class, class. Okay now, class let's settle down."

"Sophie took my crayon!" cried Maria.

"Oh yeah, well Maria broke my favorite crayon into three pieces," yelled back Sophie.

Just then Takamoto pushed Marcus off of his seat. And over by the book-shelves, Blake and José were arguing quite loudly over who would get to color the turkey for the classroom's Thanksgiving picture.

"Class, class. I said settle down," Mrs. Hale demanded.

"Mrs. Hale! Mrs.Hale!" shouted Dakota. "My great grandfather told me they used to smoke a peace pipe when everybody got mad at each other like this."

"Yes," said Mrs. Hale. "As I recall, your great grandfather was a member of a famous Indian tribe. But I believe this situation we have here today will need a different idea."

The teacher looked around the classroom and thought about her idea. She told everyone to return to their proper seat.

"Class, we are now going to have a coloring contest."

They all looked up at the teacher. They all loved to color. But Mrs. Hale said, "This coloring contest has certain rules.

"Okay. Ready? Everyone in this row, I want you to draw and then color your most favorite picture in the whole wide world…" She paused, and then added, "And only using one crayon. ***ONE CRAYON ONLY!***"

The first row looked very puzzled and did not understand.

"And I want this row to draw and color their favorite picture using ***TWO CRAYONS ONLY!***"

Row number two let out a soft low moan. "Aawwww."

"And this row," she was pointing to row number three, "I want this row to use **all ten colors in the crayon box.** We will then judge all together which row will have the best looking picture."

Analia raised her hand and asked, "Why do some kids get to use all ten colors? Their pictures will obviously be much more colorful."

The teacher answered, "At the end of this wonderful assignment, I will give all the class the answer **WHY.** But right now, let's start coloring."

Jillian whispered to herself, "Isabel over there gets to use ten colors and me only one." *Oh well*, she thought. *The teacher is very wise. She must have a good reason.*

Some time had passed and everyone seemed to be done. ***"Okay class. Time's up. Everyone hold up your pictures."*** Mrs. Hale walked up and down the rows looking at all the pictures.

"Okay class. Which row has the most colorful and detailed pictures? Which ones are the best?"

Rows number one and two quietly looked over at row number three. Row three gleamed with pride and big wide smiles. It was obvious which was best. They got to work with all ten colors.

"Class, put down your pictures," said the teacher. "I want you to look around the room and look at each other really carefully. ***Really look at every boy and girl in every seat. And take your time.***"

They didn't really understand, but they started to look around the room. It was filled with quite a variety of children. There were tall ones and skinny ones. There were heavy ones and short ones. Some kids had blue eyes and some had brown. One girl even had green eyes. Some had long pants and some had funny t-shirts. There were different colored people, too. Some had black skin and two, no three, had brown skin. Dakota was an Indian and had a little reddish skin. Some looked tan and some looked so white you could count the freckles on their face.

"Okay, class," said Mrs. Hale. Now look down at the crayons on your desk. All ten of them. Somebody tell me what will always be the best picture? The one with one color, two colors or all ten colors?"

The whole classroom shouted, "TEN COLORS!"

"Say it again, even louder."

"TEN COLORS!"

"Now look around the classroom and think of your classmates as ten colors. When you grow up, will the world be a great place to live if you can get along with one person, two persons, or all the people?"

The classroom shouted, "ALL THE PEOPLE!"

"Again class, even louder."

"ALL THE PEOPLE!"

"Get along with all the people and the world will be a beautiful picture," said the wise teacher.

"Speaking of pictures, Mrs. Hale, can we do another one, this time using all the colors?" asked Blake.

"I might have a better idea," said the teacher. And with that she brought, out a huge piece of paper that filled up most of the floor. She said very excitedly, "Why not use all the crayons and work together on one gigantic picture!"

She paused, then said jokingly, "But wait, only those who can work and play *with all the people can begin to color!*"

Not one child was left out. They all got busy working. What a beautiful picture they created together. Can you guess what the picture looked like?

THE END

A Children's Prayer

Bless me God from up above

teach me more about how to love.

Never a bad word will I say

with You there to guide my way.

Bless my family and bless my friends

and please bless me dear God until the end.

A Moment is Made

My little boy swings hard at a fast one.

A grin on his face as he conquers first base

and looking back at me

like he's king of the mountain.

They come out of nowhere

yet will last forever.

The tingles rush up from somewhere

and on any given day a moment is made.

This moment in time is locked in my mind

your wide eyed smile with mine

must be how Heaven shines.

Will you remember these days

what they were like

I pray that you might.

Lord, let me be on guard for a moment today

ready to revel in its sweet embrace

holding it tight as long as I can

never to forget its cherished face.

www.ingramcontent.com/pod-product-compliance
Lightning Source LLC
Chambersburg PA
CBHW041536240626
47164CB00002B/36